C

CW01465624

INTRODUCTION

In a world that often feels dominated by adults with their self-righteous wisdom and condescending smiles, it's easy to forget the value of truly listening to the voices of our youth. At forty-five or whatever age they deem "old", many adults believe they've cracked the code of life, their smugness over-shadowing the profound truths that can only be gleaned from those who are still navigating the turbulent waters of adolescence. But maturity is not a predetermined state; it's a conscious choice—a choice that can either bridge the gap between generations or widen it into an insurmountable chasm.

When a child reaches out for help, it is a flicker of vulnerability that deserves our attention. Instead of dismissing their struggles or offering hollow platitudes, we must guide them, empower them, and encourage them to express their thoughts and feelings freely. We must teach them that their voices matter, that their emotions are valid, and that it's okay to seek help when the weight of the world becomes too heavy to bear. Too many adults brush aside the cries for assistance, their eyes clouded by the illusion that they know better. As a result, children are often left in the shadows, where despair lurks and silence reigns.

In these moments of neglect, too many young souls turn inward, surrendering to the darkness that whispers insidiously in their ears. They give up hope, convinced that no one is willing to listen, that no one cares. And what begins as a cry for help can quickly spiral into a haunting silence that echoes through their lives, leading them down lonely roads filled with despair and self-doubt.

So, the next time a child looks to you for guidance—whether it's a fleeting question or a desperate plea—stop and listen. The act of truly hearing them might just save a life. It may even save your own, illuminating the pathways of understanding and connection that are so often overshadowed by our preconceived notions of adulthood. In a world where the youth struggle to find their voice, we must remember that listening is not just an act of kindness; it is a lifeline.

PART I

FRIDAY

1

THE TALK

The bell rang at precisely 2:45 p.m., cutting through the quiet hum of the classroom like a sharp reminder of the impending weekend. Chase watched his students filter out one by one, leaving behind a scattering of half-written notes and forgotten pencils. He gave them a nod, a weak smile, but his mind was already somewhere else—home. Home, where Reston had returned just two days ago, suitcases full of the past and all its heavy uncertainties.

"Mr. Collins, have a good weekend!" one of his students called out, pulling him back to the moment.

"You too, Jamie," Chase replied, barely hearing his own voice. The door clicked shut behind her, and the classroom was suddenly still. For a moment, Chase just stood there, staring at the empty chairs, the overhead lights casting shadows that seemed to stretch and bend in ways that felt too familiar. He glanced at the clock again. Ten minutes. He could get through this.

His phone buzzed, and instinctively, he pulled it from his pocket. A text from Liam: *Are you coming home soon?*

He stared at the message for longer than he should have, his fingers hovering over the keyboard. What could he even say? *Yes, I'm coming* or *We need to talk?* It was too much, and not enough at the same time. With a quick breath, he locked the phone and slipped it back into his pocket.

The room felt heavier now, like the weight of his thoughts had finally settled. It wasn't just about going home. It was about walking through that door and seeing Reston—Reston, who had left six months ago, saying he needed space, and now had come back without offering answers. Chase still wasn't sure if he should feel relief or dread. Maybe both.

Grabbing his bag, he left the classroom, locking the door behind him. The empty hallways echoed with the remnants of the week—locker doors clanging, muffled conversations, the slow shuffle of tired feet. It was strange how schools felt like a different world after hours, like all the energy and life that pulsed through them during the day just drained away, leaving behind nothing but silence.

By the time Chase reached his car, the sky had already started to turn dusky. He sat in the driver's seat for a moment, gripping the steering wheel and staring out at the nearly deserted parking lot. There was something peaceful about it, the way everything seemed to slow down just before the weekend really began. But for Chase, peace wasn't waiting for him at home. Only questions. Only the unresolved.

He started the engine and let the sound fill the car, drowning out the quiet that made him uneasy. As he pulled out of the lot, his thoughts returned to Reston. How they had met at a bar two years ago, the instant connection between them. How they had moved in together after only six months, because it felt right, it felt certain. How that certainty had started to crack, slowly at first, until it finally shattered the day Reston packed his things and left.

And now Reston was back. But was it the same Reston? Was he still the same Chase?

The road stretched ahead of him, a long and winding path leading to answers he wasn't sure he wanted.

THE STUDIO APARTMENT was dim when he walked in, the familiar scent of rosemary and garlic filling the air. Reston was standing by the small kitchen counter, setting two plates on the table. The sight of him there, casually putting dinner together, almost made Chase's heart ache with how normal it looked—how it had once been.

Chase dropped his bag near the door, not bothering with the usual pleasantries. He stood in the middle of the room, eyes fixed on Reston's back. "Why are you back?"

Reston didn't turn around right away. He paused, hands resting on the edge of the counter, as if the question had been expected but still hit harder than he'd prepared for. Slowly, he turned to face Chase, his expression unreadable.

"I missed you," Reston said, his voice soft, like it was a simple truth. But Chase didn't buy it. There was more. There had to be more.

"That's not an answer," Chase replied, his voice low, trying to keep the frustration from spilling over. "You left. You didn't call, didn't explain. You just walked out and now you're back. *Why?*"

RESTON RAN a hand through his hair, his face tight with something Chase couldn't quite read. "I thought I needed to be away to figure things out, but..." He trailed off, shaking his head. "I don't know, Chase. Maybe I made a mistake."

"A mistake?" Chase echoed, disbelief creeping into his tone. He took a step closer, crossing the small distance between them. "You didn't just forget to text me back, Reston. You left. Six months with nothing, and now you're here like we can just pick up where we left off?"

Reston's eyes flickered with something like guilt, but he didn't look away. "I know. I know I hurt you. I just—" He sighed, glancing down at the plates of food as if they were suddenly out of place. "I didn't know what else to do. I thought I needed space, but all it did was show me how much I needed you."

Chase crossed his arms, feeling the weight of the words but not ready to let them sink in. Not yet. "And what if I don't know if I need you back?"

Chase shook his head, pulling his hand away as if Reston had burned him. "No. You're forgetting something else. You can't just gloss over everything." He took a step back, putting some distance between them again. "The fact that you slept with Justin, my best friend. That's not something you can just erase, Reston. You can't just expect me to welcome you back like nothing happened."

Reston's face fell, and Chase could see the guilt flickering in his eyes. It was a familiar look, the one Chase had seen when they had first confronted the betrayal. "I know I messed up," Reston said, his voice strained. "I never wanted to hurt you. It just...happened. I was confused. I didn't think—"

"You didn't think?" Chase interrupted, his anger bubbling up again. "You didn't think when you jumped into bed with my best friend? You didn't think about what that would do to us? To me?" His voice rose, the memories flooding back: the pain, the betrayal, the way it felt like the ground had vanished beneath him.

"Chase, please," Reston pleaded, his expression shifting from defensiveness to desperation. "I never wanted to hurt you. That night was a mistake—a horrible mistake—and I'm not proud of it. But running away from you was worse. I thought leaving would help me find clarity, but it only made me realize how much I love you."

Chase felt a knot form in his stomach. The words sounded rehearsed, like they were plucked from a script Reston had written while he was gone. "But what about the trust?" Chase asked, his voice quieter now, almost cracking. "You broke that. You broke me. And now you want to pretend it didn't happen? You want me to forget all of it?"

Reston ran a hand through his hair, frustration and sorrow battling across his features. "I can't erase the past, Chase. I can't change what I did. I just—" He paused, taking a deep breath, as if gathering strength. "I just want a chance to show you that I've changed. That I'm willing to fight for us."

"Fight for us?" Chase echoed, incredulous. "What does that even mean? It sounds good, but it doesn't change the fact that you cheated on me and then disappeared without a word. Who do you think you are? You don't get to just walk back in and expect me to fall back in line."

Reston's eyes glistened, a mixture of regret and something more raw—vulnerability. "I know. I don't expect you to take me back. I just... I can't stand the thought of losing you for good. I want to make it up to you, but I understand if you can't forgive me. I just want you to know that I'm here now, and I want to do better."

The silence hung heavily between them, punctuated only by the faint ticking of the clock on the wall. Chase felt his chest tighten, the battle within himself raging on. Part of him wanted to reach out, to wrap Reston in his arms and pull him close, to forget the hurt. But another part—a louder part—demanded he stay strong, demanded that he not let Reston's presence erase the damage that had been done.

"You can't just keep saying that," Chase said finally, his voice steadying. "You have to show me. You have to prove that you mean it, and it's going to take more than just words."

Reston nodded, and for a moment, the fight seemed to leave him. "I will. I promise. Just give me a chance to show you."

Chase sighed, the weight of uncertainty pressing down on him again. "I don't know if I can," he admitted, his heart heavy with the truth. "It's going to take time, Reston. Time that I don't even know if we have anymore."

Reston opened his mouth to respond, but the words faltered. Chase turned away, walking toward the kitchen window, staring out at the dusk settling over the city. He felt the familiar pang of longing, but it was intertwined with a deep sense of betrayal. He wanted to believe that they could mend what was broken, but the memory of Justin's betrayal loomed like a shadow, refusing to let him forget.

Chase shook his head again, the weight of Reston's words pressing down on him like an anchor. "No," he said firmly, cutting through the tension that had settled between them. "People always say sorry. People always say it isn't you, it's me. People always say they love you but not in that same way. It's an escape. A freeing of wrongdoing, and I'm not here for it anymore."

Reston's face fell, the desperation in his eyes shifting to disbelief. "Chase—"

"No." Chase raised his voice, not out of anger but out of sheer frustration. "I'm done with the excuses. I'm done with the promises that mean nothing when they come from someone who's already broken me once. You think I can just sit here and forget what you did? You think I can let you back in just because you say you love me now? It won't be happening again in my life. Not like this."

Reston stepped back, the pain flickering across his features, but Chase felt a surge of determination wash over him. He could feel the old wounds reopening, the scars that had barely healed tearing anew. This wasn't just about Reston's betrayal; it was about his own heart, his own strength to move forward without being tethered to someone who had hurt him so deeply.

"Chase, please," Reston pleaded, his voice shaking. "I know I messed up. I just want a chance to show you that I can be better. I want to make things right between us."

Chase clenched his fists at his sides, the anger coursing through him like a river that refused to be contained. "You want to make things right? Then get the fuck out of my apartment," he said, each word punctuated with resolve. "I don't want to see you like this. I don't want to hear any more empty promises or apologies that mean nothing. You had your chance, and you threw it away."

Reston opened his mouth to protest, but Chase cut him off again. "You don't get to decide how this goes anymore. I do. And I'm done. I'm done with your apologies, your regret, and your attempts to weasel your way back into my life."

For a moment, they stood there, the air between them charged with the weight of everything unspoken. Reston's shoulders slumped, and for the first time, Chase saw something more than defiance in his eyes—he saw the reality of what he had lost.

"Chase, I'm really sorry," Reston said, his voice breaking. "I never meant to hurt you."

Chase felt the anger slowly begin to dissipate, but it was quickly replaced by something colder, more resolute. "Sorry doesn't cut it anymore, Reston. Sorry doesn't fix what's broken between us. You made your choice, and I refuse to be your safety net when it all falls apart again."

As he spoke, he turned away, glancing toward the door. He could feel the weight of Reston's presence behind him, the tension hanging like a thick fog. He took a deep breath, steadying himself, knowing he had to stand firm. He wouldn't be the one to back down this time.

"Just go," he said, his voice softer but no less commanding. "Please. Just go."

Reston hesitated, his eyes darting around the studio, taking in the memories that haunted every corner—the laughter, the late-night conversations, the love they had shared. But Chase couldn't focus on that anymore. All he could see was the hurt, the betrayal, and the man who had shattered his trust.

Finally, Reston turned, dragging his feet toward the door. Chase felt a part of him ache at the sight, but he reminded himself that this was necessary. It was time to reclaim his life, to step away from the past that had entangled him for too long.

As Reston reached for the doorknob, he paused, looking back over his shoulder. "I hope one day you can forgive me."

Chase met his gaze, his heart heavy but resolute. "I hope you find what you're looking for, Reston. Just not here."

With that, Reston stepped out, and the door clicked shut

behind him, leaving Chase alone in the dimly lit apartment. The silence settled in, wrapping around him like a familiar blanket. It felt both liberating and suffocating, and he leaned against the wall, closing his eyes.

2

WINE & POLAROIDS

R oughly thirty minutes after the door clicked shut behind Reston, Chase felt the cracks in his resolve starting to splinter. The silence in the apartment wasn't peaceful—it was deafening. Every corner of the studio, every shadow cast by the dim lamp, seemed to echo with the absence of Reston. His mind raced, his chest tightening with a pressure that felt unbearable. He had done the right thing—he knew that—but why didn't it feel like it? Why did it feel like the walls were closing in?

He sank onto the couch, his head in his hands, trying to control his breathing, but it wasn't working. His heart was still pounding in his ears, and before he could stop himself, a sob escaped his throat. It came out of nowhere, as if all the pain he had buried deep inside was now forcing its way to the surface. He didn't want to cry over Reston—not after everything—but it wasn't just about him. It was about what they had shared, what they had lost, and how it all came crashing down around him.

He couldn't sit still. He needed something, anything, to dull the ache spreading through his chest. Without thinking, he stood up and walked to the small wine rack by the window. His hands were shaking as he grabbed a bottle of red, fumbling with the corkscrew until it popped open. He didn't bother with a glass. He took a long swig straight from the bottle, the sharp taste flooding his senses. It didn't help, not really, but it gave him something else to focus on besides the suffocating grief.

His eyes darted to the closet, and he knew what he was looking for before he even took a step. The Polaroids. All the memories he had tried to bury, but never quite managed to let go of. He opened the closet door and pulled out the old shoebox from the top shelf, his breath hitching as he sat back down with it. He hesitated for a moment, staring at the box like it held a bomb about to go off.

Finally, he lifted the lid, revealing a stack of photos— fragments of a life that now felt so far away. Chase's fingers trembled as he pulled out the first Polaroid. It was from one of their first dates, back when everything had been simple. They were laughing in the photo, sitting on the grass at a park, Reston's arm draped over Chase's shoulders like they were made to fit together. He had looked so happy back then, carefree. God, he missed that version of them.

He flipped through more of the photos, each one twisting the knife a little deeper. The weekend trips to the coast, lazy mornings in bed, drunken nights where they danced in the living room, their love spilling out in messy, beautiful ways. Every snapshot was a reminder of what they once were, of what had felt so real. But now, all it did was hurt.

What did love even mean to him anymore?

Chase stared at the photos spread across the coffee table, his mind racing. He thought love was supposed to feel good, supposed to be this force that lifted you up. But all it ever seemed to do was crush him under its weight. Maybe that was his problem. Maybe he had been chasing a version of love that didn't exist, at least not for him. What was love, if not pain? How could something that was supposed to be pure twist itself into something that physically hurt?

He wiped at his eyes, feeling the sting of unshed tears. Love wasn't supposed to leave you shattered. It wasn't supposed to leave you drinking alone, sifting through old photos of a life that was gone. But here he was, wondering if any of it had been real, or if it had all been some beautiful illusion that Reston had shattered the moment he walked away.

Chase grabbed the bottle of wine again, taking another deep gulp as if it could wash away the memories. But the wine didn't dull the ache in his chest, didn't numb the raw feeling of betrayal and loss. Instead, it seemed to amplify it, the burn in his throat matching the burn in his heart.

He stared at the photos, each one blurring in his vision, and asked himself the same question over and over: Why did it hurt so much? What was it about love that made it feel like it could rip you apart from the inside out? He thought back to the nights he had spent with Reston, the way his heart had swelled with happiness, with the feeling that he had found his person. And now, that same heart felt like it was breaking, splintering into pieces he wasn't sure he could ever put back together.

The weight of it all hit him like a wave, and Chase felt himself sinking. He clutched the Polaroids in his hands, as if holding onto those memories could somehow bring back the version of love he once believed in. But deep down, he knew it was gone. Reston had taken it with him when he left.

3

REBOUND

Chase slumped further into the couch, the wine bottle nearly empty beside him, the Polaroids scattered around like ghosts from a life he barely recognized anymore. The world had softened into a blur, the edges of his pain dulling only slightly under the haze of alcohol, but the hollow ache in his chest remained, gnawing at him.

He fumbled for his phone, his vision swimming as he unlocked it. He wasn't sure why, but Aaron's name popped into his mind. His colleague, the 11th-grade English teacher, was always the laid-back one, the kind of guy who shrugged off the stresses of life with a joke or an offhand comment. Chase had always admired that about him, even envied it sometimes. Aaron didn't let things weigh him down the way Chase did. He just... lived.

As his fingers hovered over Aaron's contact, a memory flickered through his foggy brain. He remembered Aaron mentioning, in one of their late-night conversations, how one of their graduates from a handful of few years ago had become a go-go dancer. Aaron had laughed about it, saying the kid had really found his "calling" after high school, but there had been something more in the way Aaron had told the story. Like there were layers to it. He'd even joked once that the kid would do things for a fee, the insinuation clear but left hanging in the air between them.

At the time, Chase had brushed it off, uncomfortable with the idea. It seemed outlandish, something far removed from the way he lived his life. But tonight, that same idea seemed almost... daring. The boundaries of what felt reasonable were blurred, thanks to the alcohol coursing through his system. He was tired of hurting. Tired of thinking about Reston, about the lies, the betrayal, the memories that wouldn't leave him alone. Maybe he needed something to shake him out of this spiral, to remind him that there was life beyond the mess that was his broken heart.

He stared at Aaron's name on his screen, his thumb hesitating over the call button. This is crazy, he thought, but there was a spark of something in him that he hadn't felt in a long time—recklessness. It was like his emotions had been pushed to the edge, and now all he wanted was to do something, anything, that wasn't sitting here drowning in his own sorrow.

Screw it.

He tapped Aaron's name, the phone ringing in his ear, and he swayed slightly on the couch as he waited for him to pick up. After a few rings, Aaron's familiar voice came through, light and casual, as if he hadn't just been pulled into the middle of Chase's emotional breakdown.

"Chase, what's up, man?" Aaron's tone was easy, and Chase could hear the faint sounds of music in the background. "Everything okay?"

Chase blinked, trying to focus, his thoughts stumbling

over each other. "Aaron," he slurred slightly, "you remember that kid you told me about? The one who's, uh, a dancer now? Go-go dancer?"

There was a pause on the other end of the line. "Uh, yeah? Why? What about him?"

Chase let out a breath he didn't realize he was holding. He felt ridiculous saying it out loud, but the alcohol loosened his tongue. "You said... he'd do things for money, right? I mean, like, for a fee?"

Aaron chuckled, though there was a hint of surprise in his voice. "Yeah, I might've mentioned that. Why? You thinking about getting some entertainment or something?"

Chase bit his lip, leaning his head back against the couch. "I don't know," he admitted, his voice barely above a whisper. "I just...I need something, Aaron. I don't know what I'm doing anymore." He paused, the weight of his words sinking in. "Reston's gone. I told him to leave. And I don't know if I can handle being alone tonight."

There was another pause, this one longer, as if Aaron was processing what Chase had just said. When he finally spoke, his tone had softened, the usual joking edge replaced with concern. "Chase, man... are you sure this is what you want? You're going through a lot right now. Maybe this isn't the best idea."

"I don't care," Chase said, rubbing his face with his free hand. "I just want to feel something that isn't this... emptiness."

Aaron sighed on the other end of the line. "Alright, I get it. I'll send you his number. Just be careful, okay?"

Chase nodded, even though Aaron couldn't see him, his hand trembling as he lowered the phone. Moments later, a text notification popped up, and there it was—the contact. The guy's name was Will, and even through the haze of his drunken thoughts, Chase recognized it. He was one of the quieter students back then, the kind of kid you didn't think twice about in the halls. Now, his name seemed to carry a different weight.

Chase stared at the number for a long moment, the Polaroids still spread out in front of him. It felt surreal, like he was standing on the edge of something dangerous and exhilarating at the same time. He could still back out, still put his phone down and let the night pass like all the others before it. But instead, he took a deep breath, steeling himself, and started typing a message.

What was love to him, anyway? It hurt, yes. But maybe tonight, it didn't have to be about love. Maybe tonight, he could just forget.

PART II

SATURDAY

4

LANCE

I t didn't take long after Chase sent the text. Barely an hour had passed—leaving Friday night and entering into the early hours of Saturday morning—before there was a knock at the door. Chase's heart raced as he stood up from the couch, unsteady from both the wine and the nerves. He wasn't sure what he was doing, wasn't sure if this was really what he wanted, but the thought of being alone—trapped in his own head—felt unbearable.

He opened the door, and there stood Lance.

Chase blinked, taking in the sight before him. Lance looked different now—very different. He had always been good-looking, but at nineteen, he was something else entirely. The boy Chase had once taught had grown into a man, tall and broad-shouldered, his lean muscles visible under the fitted black shirt he wore. His sandy blond hair was styled messily, giving him a carefree, almost dangerous vibe. But it was his eyes that struck Chase the most—green, sharp, and knowing. Lance knew exactly why he was here.

"Hey," Lance said, his voice low and smooth as he gave Chase a once-over. "You called?"

Chase nodded, stepping aside to let him in. His apartment felt even smaller now with Lance's presence filling the space. There was an undeniable tension in the air, a charged energy that Chase hadn't expected. He'd known Lance was attractive, but standing this close to him, he realized just how much he hadn't considered it before. Maybe because he was his student back then, but now... now, Lance was something else entirely.

"Yeah, uh, thanks for coming," Chase said, trying to keep his voice steady. He closed the door behind them, leaning back against it as Lance casually surveyed the room.

"No problem," Lance replied, his eyes lingering on Chase for a moment longer than necessary. He walked further into the apartment, his movements confident, almost predatory. "So, what's going on?"

Chase swallowed, suddenly feeling self-conscious, like he was in over his head. But he had already opened this door—literally and figuratively—and there was no going back now. He pushed away the doubt and gestured vaguely at the mess of Polaroids on the coffee table, the empty wine bottle beside them.

"Reston," he muttered, trying to keep the bitterness out of his voice. "My ex. We were...we were together for a while, and he just moved back in. Thought he could walk back into my life like nothing happened. I told him to leave tonight."

Lance raised an eyebrow, his gaze flicking to the photos before coming back to Chase. "Rough."

"Yeah." Chase ran a hand through his hair, feeling the heat of embarrassment creeping up his neck. He'd never imagined himself in a situation like this, but here he was. "I just...I needed a distraction. Something to take my mind off it. Off him."

Lance smirked slightly, leaning against the edge of the

couch, his body language relaxed, but there was something dangerous about the way he looked at Chase. "A distraction, huh? I can do that."

Chase's breath hitched. There was no mistaking the intention behind Lance's words. This wasn't a casual visit. Lance knew exactly why he was here, and Chase, despite everything swirling in his head, wanted to forget—if only for one night.

Chase stepped closer, feeling his pulse quicken as the space between them shrank. Lance's eyes followed his every movement, sharp and unflinching, as if he was sizing him up. "I'm not looking for anything serious," Chase said, his voice low, almost apologetic. "I just need...something."

Lance's smirk deepened, and he pushed off the couch, closing the distance between them in a single step. He was taller than Chase remembered, more imposing now, his body heat radiating between them. "I get it," Lance said softly, his voice almost a whisper. "You want to forget about him. I can help with that."

Chase exhaled, a strange mix of anticipation and anxiety flooding his veins. He had never done anything like this before, never imagined himself calling someone for... this. But there was something freeing about it too, something that made him feel alive in a way he hadn't felt in months. Maybe even years.

Lance's hand brushed against Chase's arm, the touch light but deliberate, and Chase felt a jolt of electricity run through him. "You sure about this?" Lance asked, his voice still soft but laced with something darker, more primal.

Chase nodded, the weight of his decision settling over him like a warm blanket. "Yeah," he breathed. "I'm sure."

For a moment, they just stood there, the air between them thick with unspoken intent. Chase could feel his heart pounding in his chest, the remnants of his broken relationship with Reston fading into the background. Right now, in this moment, none of it mattered. He didn't want to think. He didn't want to hurt. He just wanted to feel something—anything—that wasn't the overwhelming emptiness Reston had left behind.

Lance's hand slid down Chase's arm, his touch firmer now, and before Chase could second-guess himself, Lance's lips were on his, urgent and demanding. It was like the floodgates had opened, and all of the pain, the confusion, the heartache, it all evaporated in the heat of that kiss.

5

ANIMALISTIC

The night had escalated in ways Chase couldn't have anticipated. The moment their clothes hit the floor, it was like a switch had flipped inside him, and before he knew it, he was lost in the heat of it all. Lance was good, no question about it—his movements confident and practiced, like he knew exactly how to pull Chase out of his head and into the moment. For a while, it worked. Chase forgot everything: Reston, the betrayal, the brokenness inside him.

But then something changed.

As Chase moved, as he let the physicality of the moment take over, something stirred deep within him. A cold, unsettling darkness crept into his chest, curling around his heart like a snake tightening its grip. He wasn't sure where it came from, but he didn't care. All that mattered was the rush it gave him. His thrusts became harder, more aggressive, and he could hear Lance's moans beneath him shift. At first, they were the usual sounds of pleasure, but then they grew strained—tinged with something else.

Pain.

And Chase...liked it.

He felt it—a sick thrill coursing through him as Lance winced, his breath catching with every rough movement. Chase's fingers dug into Lance's skin, holding him in place as he pushed harder, faster, his own ragged breath mingling with the sounds of Lance's discomfort. It was as if the pain fueled him, pushed him beyond the edge of restraint. His mind blurred with the alcohol and the raw, animalistic urge pulsing through his veins.

Lance's voice cracked, the moans of pleasure giving way to something harsher, sharper. "Chase," he managed to gasp, trying to push back. "Stop."

But Chase didn't stop. He couldn't. He didn't want to.

"Chase," Lance's voice was firmer now, panic slipping into his tone as he struggled against the weight pressing down on him. "Fuck, stop—"

Before Chase knew it, Lance's hands were on his chest, shoving him back. There was a brief moment of struggle, a chaotic blur of limbs as Lance twisted underneath him, fighting to get free. Then, out of nowhere, Lance's head snapped forward with a brutal force, and Chase didn't even see it coming.

The headbutt landed squarely on Chase's nose with a sickening crack. Pain exploded through his face, a bright white-hot flash that stole his breath. His hands flew to his face, blood pouring from his nose almost instantly, warm and sticky against his skin. He stumbled backward, completely disoriented, his vision swimming.

Before he could regain his balance, his heel caught the edge of the doorway to the bathroom, and he went down hard. The back of his skull slammed against the wooden frame with a sickening thud.

· · ·

LANCE SAT on the edge of the bed, his chest still rising and falling with the remnants of adrenaline, staring down at Chase's lifeless body. Blood trickled from Chase's nose and mouth, staining the hardwood floor beneath him. His body lay awkwardly sprawled, neck twisted at an unnatural angle, eyes glazed over. For a moment, Lance could hardly believe it—Chase was dead.

Dead.

Lance ran a hand through his hair, his fingers shaking slightly, though not from fear. He was used to this, had been for a while now. Still, this wasn't part of the plan. He hadn't come here tonight to kill anyone, especially not his old English teacher. This was supposed to be a distraction, a quick gig that would leave both of them satisfied. But when Chase had gone dark, had started hurting him, something in Lance had snapped. The headbutt hadn't been about survival —it had been instinct, muscle memory from his rough nights in the clubs. He hadn't meant for it to go this far.

But now? Now he had a problem.

Lance stood up, stretching out his muscles as he stared down at the body. He was only nineteen, but he knew what needed to be done. He'd learned it the hard way, over the past few years, running with the wrong crowd and doing jobs for people who didn't ask questions. He'd learned how to clean up messes like this. And tonight, Chase was just another mess.

"Shit," Lance muttered to himself, shaking his head. He hadn't planned for this, though. Chase wasn't some random stranger—he was someone Lance had known, someone who had taught him, someone he might have even respected once. But that didn't change the fact that Chase had crossed a line, and now there was no going back.

Lance glanced around the small studio apartment, his mind already calculating. He didn't have much time. It wouldn't be long before someone noticed something was off —maybe a neighbor would have heard the commotion, or maybe someone would wonder why Chase wasn't answering his phone. Either way, Lance knew he had to move fast.

He knelt down beside Chase's body, his expression cold and detached, and checked for a pulse—just to be sure. Nothing. Chase was definitely gone. Lance sighed, standing back up and rubbing his temples as he formulated a plan. He wasn't new to this game, but it never got easier. There was always that brief moment of guilt, the nagging voice in the back of his mind telling him he should care more.

But Lance had learned to silence that voice long ago.

"Alright," he said under his breath, steeling himself for what came next. "Time to clean this shit up."

LANCE MOVED QUICKLY, methodically. He grabbed a pair of gloves from his bag, the ones he always kept with him for situations like this, and slipped them on. He couldn't afford to leave any fingerprints. Then he started surveying the apartment, looking for anything that could link him to the scene. His eyes landed on the wine bottle, still sitting on the coffee table next to the scattered Polaroids of Chase's ex, Reston. Lance frowned, gathering the photos and tossing them into the trash. No one needed to know what had gone down here tonight—especially not Reston.

Once the photos were dealt with, Lance wiped down the wine bottle and anything else he might have touched. The apartment was small, which made things easier. He grabbed Chase's phone from the nightstand, making sure there were no messages or calls that could lead back to him. He scrolled through the recent texts, erasing the message he'd sent earlier. If anyone checked Chase's phone, there would be no trace of Lance. Unless police got involved. But, after 3 years of this, he knew they wouldn't find him.

Satisfied that he had taken care of the basics, Lance turned his attention back to the body. This was going to be the hardest part. He wasn't about to drag Chase's corpse through the building—too risky. He'd have to improvise. Luckily, he'd handled worse before.

LANCE DRAGGED Chase's limp body to the bathroom, his arms aching from the dead weight. The apartment was cramped, and every movement felt like it took more effort than it should. He let the body slump into the bathtub, the ceramic surface echoing with a dull thud. Chase's head lolled awkwardly to the side, blood still trickling from his nose, pooling around his mouth and onto the pristine white surface.

Lance stood there for a moment, staring at the body. He felt nothing—no guilt, no remorse. Just the same cold detachment that always crept in when things got messy like this. He wasn't a monster, he told himself, just someone who did what needed to be done.

Turning on his heel, he walked back to the kitchen. His boots scuffed lightly against the floor, a rhythmic sound that seemed too loud in the thick silence of the apartment. The smell of dinner still lingered in the air, a twisted reminder of what had been normal just a few hours ago. Lance could see the plates still set out on the small table, untouched, like a snapshot of a life that no longer existed.

He ignored it.

In the kitchen, his eyes settled on the butcher knife. The handle was cool against his fingers as he wrapped his hand around it, testing its weight. It would do. It would have to. He didn't have much time, and this was the only option. Chase was too big to move whole, and there was no way Lance was going to risk getting caught hauling a body out of here. He'd dealt with this kind of thing before, and as much as it turned his stomach, he knew how to make someone disappear.

Knife in hand, he walked back to the bathroom, closing the door behind him with a soft click. The apartment fell into an eerie silence, the only sound the faint hum of the refrigerator from the kitchen. Lance's breath was steady, his heart rate surprisingly calm as he stood over the tub, staring down at Chase's pale body.

"Guess this is it," Lance muttered to himself, wiping sweat from his brow. He knelt beside the tub, the butcher knife gleaming in the dim light. His hands were steady, his mind focused. He couldn't afford to screw this up—not tonight. Not ever.

The first cut was always the hardest.

The blade sank into Chase's skin with a sickening squelch, the resistance of muscle and bone sending a shiver through Lance's body. He gritted his teeth, ignoring the revulsion rising in his throat. Blood welled up, dark and thick, staining the pristine white tub as he worked. It coated his gloves, warm and sticky, as he moved methodically, separating flesh from bone with practiced precision.

It was going to be a long night.

Each slice felt like an eternity, the bathroom filling with the metallic scent of blood. Lance's muscles burned as he worked, his arms straining with the effort of cutting through bone and cartilage. Time seemed to blur, the hours passing in a haze of red and white as he dismembered the body piece by piece.

By the time he was done, the tub was filled with blood, the body reduced to nothing more than parts that would be easier to dispose of. Lance sat back on his heels, wiping a streak of blood from his cheek with the back of his glove. His breathing was heavy, his body sore, but the job was done.

Now came the next part—the cleanup. He'd need to be quick, thorough, and leave no trace behind. There couldn't be any evidence. No one could ever know that Lance had once been here.

Lance glanced at the bathroom door, the faint light from the apartment spilling in under the crack. The night was far from over.

LANCE STOOD UP, feeling the tightness in his back and shoulders as he walked back to the kitchen. His hands trembled slightly, the adrenaline still coursing through his veins. He opened the cabinet under the sink and pulled out a box of heavy-duty garbage bags, tearing one off the roll and shaking it open with a sharp snap. He returned to the bathroom, the smell of blood heavy in the air as he began stuffing Chase's dismembered remains into the plastic.

Piece by piece, he filled the bag, tying it tightly once it was full. He repeated the process, methodically packing the other parts into more bags, careful to avoid any splatters or leaks. The weight of the bags was heavy, but manageable. The hardest part was done, but he knew that if he didn't handle the rest perfectly, it would all fall apart.

He turned to the blood-soaked tub. For a moment, the sheer amount of blood made him pause, but he had no time to reflect on it. Lance grabbed a towel and wiped his gloved hands before taking out a bottle of bleach from beneath the sink. He poured it liberally over the tub, the harsh chemical smell mixing with the iron scent of blood. He scrubbed vigorously, wiping away the last traces of what had been Chase. The floor, the tiles, the tub—everything needed to be spotless.

It took him longer than he'd expected, his muscles burning with exhaustion, but finally, the room gleamed under the dim light. Not a drop of blood remained. The bathroom was clean, sterile, as if nothing had ever happened.

Satisfied, Lance stood up, wiped the sweat from his fore-head, and removed the gloves, stuffing them into the last garbage bag. He glanced around the room one last time, making sure he hadn't overlooked anything. He couldn't afford a single mistake.

Then he noticed the small window above the bathtub.

The alleyway outside was dark and narrow, mostly hidden from view. It was perfect—no one would see him if he was quick. Lance pushed the window open, cold air rushing in. He grabbed the garbage bags, hoisting them one by one over the tub and through the window. They landed with dull thuds in the alley below, hidden in the shadows.

Climbing onto the edge of the tub, Lance leaned out the window, scanning the alley. It was empty, just as he'd hoped. The bags were barely visible in the dim light from the street-lamps, blending into the darkness. He could get rid of them without anyone noticing.

He climbed back down, gave the bathroom one final sweep with his eyes, and then stepped out into the living room. The plates were still on the table, the smell of the uneaten dinner still hanging in the air. Lance felt a strange, hollow sensation in his chest as he grabbed his bag and headed for the door.

The apartment was silent as he locked the door behind him, the weight of everything he'd done hanging in the air. He could feel the tension in his body, the exhaustion setting in, but there was no time to stop. He had to finish this.

Out in the alley, the night air was cool, the city around him quiet. Lance approached the bags, crouching down to gather them in his arms. They were heavy, awkward, but he managed to hold them all at once. He glanced around the alley again, making sure no one was watching.

It was time to disappear.

PART III

SUNDAY

6

DUMPING

The highway stretched out like a black ribbon beneath the starlit sky, punctuated only by the occasional flicker of headlights in the distance. The soft hum of the Mustang's engine was soothing as Lance drove deeper into the heart of Georgia. The open stretch of road felt both liberating and suffocating; he was free to escape, yet the weight of what he had done loomed heavy in the back of his mind.

Around three in the morning, now Sunday, he spotted a rest area ahead. Pulling off the highway, he parked in the shadows, the faint light of the moon illuminating the dense trees that surrounded him. The air was thick and humid, clinging to his skin as he stepped out of the car. Lance approached the trunk of his Mustang, the metal cool to the touch as he opened it.

His heart raced as he looked at the heavy garbage bags sitting inside, a stark reminder of the night's events. He swallowed hard, fighting the nausea rising in his throat. This wasn't just trash; it was evidence of a life he had taken. For a brief moment, he hesitated, but the urgency to dispose of the bags pushed him forward. He had to rid himself of the past, even if it meant embracing the darkness that came with it.

With quick, practiced motions, he grabbed the bags and made his way toward the edge of the nearby swamp. The moonlight shimmered off the water, creating a ghostly glow that seemed to beckon him closer. Lance felt a primal thrill as he tossed the bags into the murky depths. They hit the water with a heavy splash, sinking into the darkness like they'd never existed at all.

A couple of alligators floated nearby, their eyes gleaming like ominous pearls in the dim light. Lance couldn't help but shiver as he imagined them feasting on the contents of the bags. "Just another day in the life," he muttered under his breath, feeling a strange mix of dread and exhilaration.

He stepped back, wiping his palms on his jeans, trying to shake off the creeping sensation of horror that settled in his chest. The swamp was eerily quiet, the sounds of nature punctuated only by the distant croak of frogs and the occasional rustle of leaves. He took a moment to collect himself, breathing in the thick, humid air as he fought to push the memory of Chase from his mind.

But it lingered, a specter that wouldn't fade away.

After a moment, he turned back to his Mustang, the weight of his decision hanging heavy in the air. He slid back into the driver's seat, feeling the familiar rumble of the engine beneath him. He took a deep breath, trying to clear his mind of the chaos that had just unfolded. There was no turning back now. He glanced in the rearview mirror, watching the swamp fade into the distance as he pulled back onto the highway.

With the gas pedal pressed firmly to the floor, Lance picked up speed, the wind whipping through the open windows. The further he drove, the more he felt the tension within him ease. Not much longer now, he thought, the thought of Justin and the sandy beaches of Florida drawing him forward.

As the sun began to rise in the distance, painting the sky with streaks of pink and orange, he found solace in the rhythm of the road. The car became an extension of himself, a vessel carrying him away from the darkness and towards a future that remained uncertain but was filled with possibilities. The moment of reckoning would come, but for now, he let the landscape blur past him, lost in the promise of escape.

7

SUNNY BEACH

T he heat of Miami hit Lance like a wall the moment he stepped out of his Mustang. The salty breeze, the bright sun, and the energy of the city all collided in a way that felt surreal after the long, tense drive. He took a moment to compose himself, pulling his sunglasses down over his eyes before heading toward the small café where Justin had told him to meet.

When Lance arrived, Justin was already there, casually lounging at a table on the sidewalk patio, sipping a mimosa and scrolling through his phone. Dressed in a loose white linen shirt and designer sunglasses, Justin looked like he belonged here—effortlessly stylish, cool, and totally at ease with the world around him. It was the complete opposite of how Lance felt, still raw from what he'd done the night before.

"About time, man," Justin said with a grin, raising his glass. "I was starting to think you bailed on me."

Lance forced a smile as he slid into the seat across from him. "Nah, just needed to clean up a few things before I got here."

Justin raised an eyebrow but didn't press for details. "Well, you're here now. Let's enjoy the day. Brunch is on me." He waved over the waiter and ordered another round of mimosas, along with a spread of food that looked like it could feed a small army.

The conversation started off light, Justin filling Lance in on his life in Miami—how the parties were endless, the people were beautiful, and the opportunities for fun seemed to come knocking every night. Lance nodded along, trying to lose himself in the mundane details, but the weight of his actions clung to him, dark and unshakable.

Eventually, after the first few sips of his drink, Lance leaned forward, his voice dropping just above a whisper. "Justin... I need to tell you something."

Justin barely looked up from his mimosa, giving only a casual shrug. "What? You murdered someone or something?"

Lance blinked, caught off guard by the nonchalance in his friend's voice. "Yeah," he said, testing the waters, "actually, I did."

That got Justin's attention. He raised an eyebrow and slowly set his glass down, but there was no shock in his eyes —just mild curiosity. "Who?"

"My old English teacher, Mr. Collins. Last night. I didn't mean for it to happen, but... it did."

For a moment, there was silence between them, the sounds of clinking silverware and idle conversation filling the air around them. Lance waited for a reaction, for some sign that what he had just admitted was sinking in, but Justin remained cool as ever.

Then, Justin leaned back in his chair, a small smile tugging at the corner of his lips. "Well," he said, "I guess that's one way to take control of a situation."

Lance stared at him, unsure of how to respond. "You're not...I don't know...freaked out? At all?"

Justin laughed, a light, carefree sound that seemed out of place given the gravity of the situation. "Why would I be? Look, Lance, you've got to stop thinking that everyone else's rules apply to you. You're the main character of this life. Everyone else? They're just extras. Disposable, replaceable. You do what you need to do, and don't let anyone make you feel bad about it."

Lance felt his heart race, a strange mixture of relief and unease settling over him. The way Justin said it—so calmly, so easily—it made it all seem... normal. Like what he had done wasn't some horrific crime but just another step in taking control of his life.

Justin continued, leaning forward now, his voice conspiratorial. "You think anyone cares about Chase? No. You're here, in Miami, living your life. This is your story, Lance. Don't get hung up on the details. It's all about moving forward."

Lance swallowed hard, feeling the words sink into him. He'd always admired Justin's carefree attitude, the way he seemed to glide through life without ever getting weighed down by the consequences of his actions. But now, in this moment, it felt like more than just an attitude—it felt like permission. Permission to keep moving forward, to leave the past behind and never look back.

"You're right," Lance said slowly, the weight on his shoulders beginning to lift. "I've been overthinking it."

Justin smiled again, raising his glass. "Exactly. So stop overthinking. We've got a whole day ahead of us, and you're in Miami, baby. Time to live."

Lance clinked his glass against Justin's, feeling a strange sense of clarity wash over him. The road ahead, once filled with uncertainty, suddenly seemed a lot clearer. He was in control now. This was his story, and he was done playing by anyone else's rules.

THE SUN WAS BEGINNING to sink over Miami, casting the streets in a warm, orange glow as Lance drove his Mustang through the busy city streets with Justin beside him. The rumble of the engine and the steady hum of conversation on the radio created a strange sense of calm in Lance, but beneath that calm, something else lingered. Something dark, something unsettling.

Justin was leaning back in the passenger seat, his sunglasses reflecting the bright lights of South Beach as they neared his condo. "This is going to be wild, man," Justin said with a grin, tapping Lance's dashboard in excitement. "You'll get to meet some of the best in the business. Trust me, these guys know how to party."

Lance forced a smile, though a strange unease tugged at the edges of his mind. He hadn't been able to shake the feeling ever since their conversation at brunch. Justin had been so nonchalant about everything—so dismissive of Chase's death, of what Lance had done. And while a part of Lance had found comfort in that, another part of him couldn't help but wonder if something was wrong. Or maybe it wasn't just wrong. Maybe it was all in his head.

They pulled into the parking garage under Justin's condo, the sleek building towering over them, gleaming in the last light of the day. Lance killed the engine and sat for a moment, his hand still gripping the steering wheel tightly. He glanced over at Justin, who was already out of the car, motioning for him to hurry up.

"Let's go, man! We've got work to do if we're gonna get

this place ready," Justin called out, his voice echoing in the garage.

Lance got out, following Justin to the elevator that led up to the condo. As they rode up in silence, he found his thoughts drifting, his mind returning to the events of the previous night. The look on Chase's face, the way it all spiraled so quickly. And Justin's reaction—wasn't it strange? The way he brushed it off so casually? Or maybe it was just Justin being Justin. Lance shook his head, trying to shake the thoughts away, but they stuck to him like a persistent shadow.

Justin's condo was a minimalist masterpiece—clean lines, white walls, floor-to-ceiling windows with a view of the beach. As they entered, Justin immediately started barking orders, directing Lance toward boxes of decorations and supplies for the party. Lance began unpacking, hanging up streamers and setting up tables, but his mind wasn't entirely focused on the task.

As he worked, something odd caught his eye. He glanced up at Justin, who was meticulously arranging drinks on the counter. For a split second, Justin's figure seemed to shimmer, like a mirage under the harsh condo lights. Lance blinked, his vision clearing, but the moment left him feeling unsettled. His heart beat a little faster, his breath coming in shallow bursts.

He rubbed his eyes and got back to work, telling himself it was just exhaustion—maybe even the residual effects of the wine from last night. But as they continued setting up for the party, the feeling only grew. Justin's voice seemed distant at times, as though coming from far away, even though he was right in front of Lance. The light in the condo seemed too bright, too harsh, casting strange shadows that didn't quite match up with where the furniture was.

Justin turned to him suddenly, holding up a bottle of champagne. "You ready for tonight? This is going to be epic."

Lance nodded, but his hands felt cold, clammy. He looked at Justin, really looked at him, and for the first time, he felt a sliver of doubt snake its way into his thoughts. Something was off. The way Justin moved, the way his voice echoed, the way he seemed to shift in and out of focus like a glitch in reality. Was Justin even real?

"Yeah," Lance said, his voice hollow, barely above a whisper.

Justin grinned, not noticing Lance's growing discomfort, or maybe he didn't care. "Don't be so tense. This is what you came here for. Let loose. Live your life."

Lance swallowed hard, a chill running down his spine. He turned back to the table, his hands trembling slightly as he set out the last of the decorations. But he couldn't stop glancing at Justin, at the way he seemed too perfect, too present, yet somehow... not.

As the evening crept closer and the sun dipped below the horizon, Lance felt the pressure building inside him. The cracks in his sanity were beginning to show. He couldn't tell if it was the guilt of what he'd done, or if there was something else —something more sinister lurking just below the surface of his mind. Either way, the walls around him seemed to be closing in.

Justin clapped his hands together, pulling Lance from his thoughts. "Alright, everything's ready. Let's get changed. People will be here any minute." He motioned toward the bedroom, his grin wide and easy.

Lance nodded again, mechanically moving toward the

bedroom to change. But as he glanced at his reflection in the mirror, a cold sweat broke out on his skin. His face looked pale, his eyes wild. And in the corner of the mirror, just out of sight, Justin's figure flickered once again, barely there, like a shadow or an illusion.

Was Justin real? Or was this something else?

As the sun fully dipped below the horizon and night swallowed South Beach in neon lights and endless music, Justin's clients began to arrive. One by one, they strolled into the condo, a mix of lean, muscular bodies and barely-there outfits, all of them go-go dancers who worked the clubs and private events that Justin was known for organizing. The music started low at first—something with a sultry, throbbing beat that seemed to vibrate through the walls.

Lance poured himself a drink, trying to shake off the lingering unease from earlier. He could feel the room filling up around him, bodies brushing against each other as people laughed and mingled, their voices blending into a chaotic symphony. Justin was in his element, moving through the crowd with ease, greeting people, making small talk, and keeping the energy alive. Lance, on the other hand, was already three drinks deep, and the alcohol had started to buzz through his veins.

He found himself leaning against the counter, watching the party unfold. A couple of the dancers caught his eye—a tall, dark-haired guy with striking tattoos and a shorter, blonde one with an infectious smile. The alcohol loosened his inhibitions, and before long, he was flirting with both of them, their conversations playful, suggestive. He could feel their eyes lingering on him, their touches lingering just a bit too long.

But every time he glanced over at Justin, he felt that strange pull again, that sense that something wasn't quite right. Justin would lock eyes with him across the room and smile, a smile that seemed too knowing, too present. It was as though Justin was waiting for something, but Lance couldn't tell what.

Eventually, Justin appeared beside him, his hand resting on Lance's shoulder. "You're making quite the impression," he said, his voice smooth as ever. "But hey, before things get too crazy, I want you to do something for me."

Lance raised an eyebrow, the alcohol making his thoughts feel sluggish. "What's that?"

Justin leaned in, his smile widening. "Give a speech. About your move to South Beach. About your new life here. These guys respect you, you know? They see you as part of the crew now."

Lance blinked, the request catching him off guard. "A speech? I'm not really—"

Justin cut him off with a wink. "Trust me, it'll be great. They need to hear from you. Besides, you've had enough to drink to make it fun." He gestured toward the room, where the music had shifted into something louder, the bass thumping hard. "Go on, you've got this."

Before Lance could protest, Justin clapped his hands, drawing the attention of the party. "Everyone! Everyone, quiet down for a sec!" he called out, his voice cutting through the noise like a knife. The room gradually fell silent, all eyes turning to Lance.

Lance swallowed hard, the pressure of so many eyes making him feel exposed. He grabbed his drink and downed the rest of it, hoping the alcohol would give him the confidence he needed. As he stepped forward, the crowd parted slightly, giving him space to speak. His mind swirled with thoughts—of Chase, of the body in the swamp, of Justin's strange, shimmering presence that continued to haunt him.

"Uh, hey, everyone," Lance started, his voice sounding strange to his own ears. "So, I guess Justin wanted me to say a few words. I, uh, just moved here, as some of you know. I wasn't really sure what to expect, but South Beach has been... well, it's been something." He chuckled nervously, and a few people in the crowd laughed with him, though their laughter sounded hollow.

He continued, the words stumbling out of him. "I've been through a lot recently. But coming here, being part of this new scene, it's like I'm finally free to live how I want. No more baggage, no more bullshit. Just... freedom."

As he spoke, something strange began to happen. The room, which had been filled with casual smiles and nods of encouragement, started to shift. The faces in the crowd twisted, slowly at first, but then more dramatically. Their expressions became exaggerated, their smiles too wide, their eyes too bright, as if something dark was leaking out from behind their masks.

Lance blinked, feeling a sudden wave of vertigo. The people in front of him—these men, who only moments ago seemed like regular partygoers—were now staring at him with an intensity that made his skin crawl. Their faces seemed to stretch, their teeth bared in grotesque grins that looked more like snarls. He could hear them whispering to each other, low and guttural, though the words didn't make any sense.

His heart raced as the crowd began to edge closer, their movements sharp, predatory. One of them—a guy with a shaved head and dark eyes—stepped forward, his hand twitching as though it was preparing to strike. Lance's pulse quickened, a cold sweat breaking out on his skin. He felt trapped, the room closing in on him, the once-familiar faces now warped into something out of a nightmare.

Justin stood off to the side, watching the whole scene unfold, his expression unchanged. He didn't move to stop them. He didn't say anything at all. Just stood there, smiling.

"What... what is this?" Lance stammered, stepping back as the crowd pressed closer. His voice shook, the panic rising in his throat.

"Relax, Lance," Justin finally said, his voice smooth but distant, like it was coming from underwater. "This is your new life. This is what you wanted."

Lance's breath came in short, shallow bursts, his vision blurring as the room around him seemed to spin. The music was deafening now, pounding in his ears, drowning out his thoughts. He tried to back away, but the crowd was relentless, closing in, their hands reaching for him, their eyes glinting with something he couldn't quite place—violence, hunger, something primal.

And then, just as his panic reached its peak, everything stopped. The crowd froze, the music cut out, and the room plunged into an eerie silence.

Lance blinked, his heart still racing, his body trembling. When he looked up, Justin was gone. And the people—those twisted, snarling faces—were nothing more than shadows now, fading into the corners of the room as though they had never been there at all.

8

SHADOWS & LIES

L ance woke up to a pounding headache and the overwhelming stench of stale liquor and sweat. He groaned as he sat up on the couch, blinking against the harsh light streaming in through the windows. The condo was a wreck—bottles tipped over, half-empty glasses scattered across every surface, and the faint smell of something burning in the kitchen. His head throbbed as he tried to piece together what had happened last night, but everything felt like a blur.

He scanned the room, searching for any sign of Justin, but the place was eerily quiet. No music, no voices, no laughter. The air felt thick with a strange tension. Lance ran a hand through his hair, trying to shake off the dizziness. He remembered the party, the faces warping, the crowd closing in on him, and Justin pushing him to give that speech. But after that? His memory turned into a mess of flashes— shadowy faces, whispers that didn't make sense, and that awful, creeping feeling that something was very wrong.

Standing up, Lance stumbled through the condo, his

feet dragging across the hardwood floors. As he moved from room to room, a sense of unease settled deep in his gut. Was this even his place? He could barely remember how he ended up here. His mind felt foggy, like he was trying to wade through a dream that wouldn't quite let him go.

The bedroom door was slightly ajar, and he hesitated before pushing it open. Inside, the bed was unmade, sheets rumpled and pillows thrown haphazardly across the floor. But it wasn't the state of the room that made him stop—it was the photographs on the dresser.

Lance walked over slowly, his heart pounding harder in his chest. The photos were of him...and someone else. Some guy. They looked happy in the pictures, smiling, arms around each other. There were snapshots of them at the beach, laughing at a bar, one of them dressed in tuxedos as if for a wedding. Lance stared at the images, his mind reeling. He didn't remember this. He didn't remember any of it.

But there they were—clear as day. Him and this guy, like they'd been together for years.

He felt a chill crawl up his spine as he looked closer at the pictures. In each one, they were wearing matching rings. Lance's gaze dropped to the bedside table, and that's when he saw it. A wedding ring, sitting alone, glinting under the soft light of the lamp.

Lance picked it up, his hands shaking. He turned it over in his fingers, the weight of it familiar but foreign at the same time. His chest tightened, his breath quickening. He didn't understand what any of this meant.

Who was the *guy* in the pictures?

Who was *he* supposed to be?

. . .

LANCE'S PHONE BUZZED, jolting him from his daze. He glanced down and saw the screen light up—nine missed calls from the same number. The name didn't register, just a number staring back at him. His heart raced as he hesitated before answering. He swiped to accept the call, bringing the phone to his ear.

"Hello?" Lance's voice was hoarse, shaky.

"Lance? Oh my God, where the hell have you been?" The voice on the other end was frantic, a mix of panic and relief. "It's been almost six months, I thought—Jesus, I thought you were dead. I've been looking for you everywhere."

Lance blinked, trying to make sense of the words, but his head still felt clouded, weighed down by the remnants of last night. "Who is this?" he asked, his voice rough, unsure.

There was a pause, the person on the other end letting out a sharp breath, almost like they were trying to process his question. "What do you mean, who is this? It's Justin. Lance, it's me—Justin."

Lance's mouth went dry. He let out a half-laugh, the confusion settling in deeper. "No, that's not possible. You were here last night. I was with you, Justin. At the party, remember? You made me give that speech..."

There was another pause, this one longer. The voice on the other end softened, full of disbelief. "Lance, I haven't seen you in *months*. That wasn't me. I've been working with the police trying to figure out where you've been. We thought you were missing, babe. You just disappeared."

Lance's mind spun. His pulse thudded loudly in his ears as he tried to reconcile what he was hearing. None of it made any sense. "I don't know who the hell you are," Lance muttered, feeling a creeping dread inch up his spine. He glanced back at the pictures on the dresser, the faces staring at him like they knew something he didn't. "How can you be Justin? You were just here. I—"

"Lance," Justin's voice broke through his spiral, firmer this time. "Look at the wedding picture. On the dresser. You remember the rehearsal dinner before we got married, right? I wore that stupid blue tie you hated."

Lance's breath caught in his throat. His eyes flicked down to one of the framed photos. It was of him and the man—Justin—smiling, arms around each other, both of them in formal suits, the blue tie standing out. His stomach churned.

"This...this can't be real," Lance whispered. His fingers trembled as he held the phone to his ear, staring at the image that didn't feel like his life. But it was there. The proof. His mind reeled, flashing between the distorted faces from last night, the twisted party, and the fact that none of it added up. "I don't remember this," Lance mumbled. "I don't remember you."

The silence on the other end of the call was heavy, and when Justin spoke again, his voice was thick with pain. "Lance, you've been missing for months. I don't know what's happened to you, but I swear to God, we'll figure it out. You're scaring the hell out of me."

Lance's heart pounded against his ribs, fear and confusion battling inside him. The ring in his hand felt cold, almost foreign. He was holding a life he didn't remember, but it was *his* life. Or was it?

Then, Justin mentioned something that made his heart skip a beat.

· · ·

LANCE'S BREATHING grew shallow as Justin's words sunk in. His pulse roared in his ears, and his fingers tightened around the phone, the truth slowly uncoiling in his mind like a serpent waking from slumber.

"We ran into him? My stepbrother?" Lance's voice was barely a whisper, the words catching in his throat.

"Yeah," Justin replied, his voice carrying the weight of old pain. "We were out one night. Some random place—I don't even remember where. And then you just froze. I didn't know what was going on until I saw him. He looked right at you, like he was...I don't know, like he was daring you to react."

Lance's heart twisted violently in his chest. A rush of nausea hit him, memories flooding back in bits and pieces —the cold, slick fear, the way his body had gone numb at the sight of his stepbrother's face. He hadn't seen him in years, hadn't spoken his name, but in that moment, everything came crashing back. All the nightmares, the shame, the anger he thought he'd buried.

"Jesus," Lance breathed, his voice barely audible. "I don't...I didn't remember."

"You freaked out, Lance," Justin continued, his voice quieter now, gentler. "I tried to help. I tried to calm you down, but it was like something snapped in you. You pushed me away. Said you couldn't deal with it, and you just...disappeared. Like you weren't even you anymore."

Lance's legs felt weak, and he stumbled back, sitting heavily on the bed. The wedding ring he'd been holding slipped from his fingers and rolled onto the floor, but he barely noticed. The weight of Justin's words pressed down on him, crushing him from all sides.

"I don't remember any of this," Lance muttered, his mind spinning. "I just...I can't..."

"You don't remember because you didn't want to," Justin said softly. "It broke something in you, Lance. That night, seeing him again I think it tore open all those old wounds, and you didn't know how to deal with it. So you ran. You've been running ever since."

Lance felt the walls closing in on him, his breath coming in shallow, ragged bursts. His past, which he had spent years trying to bury, had caught up with him. The shame, the helplessness, the fear—it all came rushing back, overwhelming him.

"I don't know who I am anymore," Lance whispered, tears welling in his eyes as he stared down at the floor, his whole body trembling. "I don't know what's real, what's... what's me."

There was silence on the other end for a moment, and then Justin spoke, his voice full of compassion but steady. "You're still you, Lance. You're hurt. You're lost. But you're still you. We can figure this out. We'll get through this. But you've gotta come back. You've gotta let me help."

Lance wiped at his face, his hands shaking as he tried to steady himself. Justin's words were a lifeline, but the storm raging inside him felt too powerful to be contained.

LANCE'S HEART raced as Justin's voice came through the line again, more urgent this time. "I'm at the police station right now, trying to figure this out. I'll head back to the condo as soon as I can. Just stay there, okay? Don't do anything crazy."

The words echoed in Lance's ears as they hung up. But something in the way Justin spoke—it didn't sit right. His gut twisted, and suddenly, he was sure. Justin wasn't coming back alone. The police were coming for him.

Panic surged through Lance. His mind buzzed with fear, every thought scrambled and wild. He needed to protect himself. He needed something—anything—to hold off whatever was about to happen. His breath came fast and shallow as he stumbled through the condo, eyes darting to every corner, searching for a weapon.

He stormed into the living room first, ripping through drawers, pulling cushions off the couch—nothing. His hands were shaking as he shoved open the door to the dining area, scanning the space, but it was bare. His mind screamed, and sweat dripped down his forehead as he spun on his heel, heading straight for the kitchen.

The air felt heavy, suffocating, as he yanked open cabinets and drawers, tossing aside pots, pans, and utensils. Then, out of the corner of his eye, he spotted something in the dish rack. His pulse quickened as he darted toward it—a meat pounder. It was heavy, the solid steel handle cold in his hand.

Lance gripped it tightly, feeling the weight of it as his breath came in ragged bursts. This was it. His only chance. His only way to survive whatever was about to happen.

Without thinking, Lance rushed toward the balcony door, his footsteps loud against the tiled floor. He slid the door open just enough to slip through, crouching low behind the outdoor furniture, his heart thundering in his chest. The night air was thick and humid, clinging to his skin as he waited, the meat pounder clenched tightly in his trembling hand.

His eyes darted back toward the sliding door, waiting for any sound, any movement. He could feel the darkness closing in around him, the weight of his own paranoia pressing down harder with every second. *Were they coming? Was Justin lying?* His mind spun in a blur of fear and doubt.

Lance's grip tightened on the handle of the meat pounder as he crouched lower behind the balcony railing. The distant hum of the city streets below faded into the background. All that mattered was the moment ahead—*survive.*

9

AVOIDANCE

Lance's heart pounded in his chest as he crouched behind the balcony furniture, gripping the meat pounder like a lifeline. The sound of the front door opening sent a jolt of adrenaline through his body. He heard the soft shuffle of multiple feet, barely audible, but unmistakable—someone was inside. They were moving quietly, as if trying not to startle him.

Then, a voice broke the silence. It wasn't Justin's.

"This is Dr. Harris. I'm a psychologist with the city of Miami," the voice said, calm and measured. "Lance, we're here to help. No one wants to hurt you. Let's figure this out together."

Lance's mind reeled. A psychologist? Why would they send a psychologist? His grip tightened on the meat pounder, his palms slick with sweat. He pressed his back against the cold railing, his breaths shallow and ragged as the footsteps moved around the condo. They were searching for him, moving closer to the balcony with each passing second.

His body went rigid when he heard the footsteps

nearing the sliding glass door. Panic gripped him. He couldn't think—he couldn't breathe. They were going to find him. They were going to take him.

Without thinking, Lance exploded from his hiding spot, the meat pounder raised high in the air. He swung with all his strength, the desperation fueling him, but his aim was wild. Instead of connecting with the figure moving toward the balcony, the heavy steel slammed into the glass door with a sickening crack.

The sound echoed in the night air as a deep, jagged crack spread across the glass like a spiderweb. Lance stumbled back, his chest heaving as he stared at the door, the realization of what he'd done sinking in. His ears rang from the force of the impact, and his hands trembled violently around the handle of the meat pounder.

"Lance, stop!" the woman's voice called out again, this time more urgent but still calm. "We're not here to hurt you. Please, just talk to me."

But all Lance could hear was the sound of his own heartbeat, the crack in the glass looming in front of him like a fracture in his reality. The footsteps hesitated, and he could feel them watching him through the glass, waiting for his next move.

He didn't have a plan. He didn't know what he was doing anymore. All he knew was that he couldn't go back inside. He couldn't face whatever was waiting for him beyond that door. His grip on the meat pounder faltered, and for a brief moment, his entire body felt weightless, like he was floating in a sea of uncertainty.

What had he done?

. . .

DR. HARRIS'S voice broke through the fog in Lance's mind, steady but gentle, like someone trying to reach a lost child. "Lance, do you remember when we first met? It was three years ago. You'd just started college here in Miami. You were excited to get away, but then... you ran into your stepbrother, and everything changed. Do you remember that?"

Lance's pulse throbbed in his ears, and he gripped the meat pounder tighter, his knuckles turning white. "That's not true," he spat, his voice cracking with a mixture of anger and confusion. "I wouldn't run. I don't run from anything. I'm not...I'm not scared."

But even as the words left his mouth, they felt hollow. He wasn't sure of anything anymore. His mind was spinning, unraveling, the truth blurring with the lies he'd told himself for years. He could barely remember what was real.

Dr. Harris didn't push, but her voice softened as she continued. "It's normal to want to escape, Lance, especially after what happened to you. What you went through was unimaginable. You were trying to protect yourself the only way you knew how. Avoidance Personality Disorder, that's what we've been working through since you came to me. It's a coping mechanism. Your mind wants to avoid the truth, the pain, because it's too much to bear. But it's not your fault."

Lance shook his head violently, his vision swimming as he backed away from the cracked glass door. His heart hammered against his ribs, and a sharp pain bloomed in his chest. "No, you're wrong! I wouldn't...I wouldn't just run away. I'm not weak!"

"You're not weak, Lance," Dr. Harris said firmly, taking a cautious step closer to the door, her shadow outlined in the fractured glass. "This isn't about weakness. This is about surviving. You've been running because it's the only way you've known how to survive. But you don't have to keep running. Not anymore."

Lance's body trembled as the words hit him. He wanted to believe her, but his mind was a tangled mess of memories and half-truths, and nothing made sense anymore. He couldn't even remember when things had started falling apart. "I don't know what's real," he muttered, his voice barely a whisper. "I don't even know who I am anymore."

"You're Lance," Dr. Harris replied gently. "You're the same person you've always been. You're the person who's been trying to survive in the only way he knew how. But it's time to stop running. It's time to face the truth, no matter how hard it is."

Lance let out a shaky breath, his head swimming. He couldn't tell if she was right or if this was just another trick his mind was playing on him. He felt like he was slipping through the cracks, losing himself in the chaos.

"Lance, you're not alone in this," Dr. Harris said, her voice still warm and welcoming. "You've got people who care about you. Justin cares about you. He's been trying to find you, to help you. But we need you to let us in. We need you to stop running."

Her words echoed in his mind, each one tugging at the walls he had built around himself. He had been running— maybe for longer than he realized. But how could he stop? How could he face everything he'd buried deep inside?

"No," he whispered, the word a fragile breath. "No, I...I can't. I don't...I can't face it."

Dr. Harris took another step closer, her silhouette clearer now through the cracked door. "You can. And you don't have to do it alone."

· · ·

LANCE'S EYES widened as he saw Dr. Harris inching closer, her calm presence now suffocating him. His chest tightened, and a cold sweat trickled down his back. He couldn't take the pressure—he wasn't ready. Not for this.

"Back up!" he screamed, his voice trembling as he took another shaky step toward the far side of the balcony. "Don't...don't pressure me!"

Dr. Harris froze mid-step, her eyes locked on him, but she didn't say anything. She was trying to remain calm, Lance knew that. But then, just behind her, he spotted someone else—tall, dressed in black, and carrying a weapon. His heart rate spiked. It looked like a SWAT officer.

"No!" Lance shouted again, waving the meat pounder in the air, his movements frantic. "Tell them to leave! I'm not coming out until they're gone! Get them out of here!"

His mind raced as he watched Dr. Harris glance over her shoulder at the figure behind her. For a moment, there was silence, but the tension in the air was thick. Lance could feel his grip on reality slipping further with each passing second. He couldn't trust anyone, not even her—not while they were all here. He stood up from behind the furniture.

"I mean it!" Lance yelled, his voice hoarse. "I'm not coming out until they leave."

Dr. Harris raised her hand slowly, motioning for the officer to step back. Her gaze never left Lance's, and after a few seconds, the shadow of the SWAT officer began to retreat, disappearing out of Lance's view.

The silence that followed was deafening.

For a long moment, Lance just stood there, gripping the meat pounder so hard his hands ached. His thoughts churned, his mind spinning in a million directions at once. He didn't know what to do. Didn't know who to trust. But one thing was clear: he couldn't let them take him. Not like this.

Finally, he took a deep, shaky breath and pointed at Dr. Harris. "You. Only you stay. Everyone else...gone."

Dr. Harris nodded slowly, her movements deliberate. She seemed to understand that any wrong move could set him off again. "Okay, Lance," she said softly. "I'm the only one here now. No one else."

Lance watched her closely, his mind a maze of fear and confusion. He wanted to believe her, but paranoia twisted in his gut, making him second-guess everything. He had no way of knowing if she was telling the truth. He felt trapped, his thoughts running wild.

"Show me," he muttered. His voice was weak but demanding. "I need to see them leave. All of them."

Dr. Harris didn't argue. She stepped back, her hands visible, and moved toward the front door of the condo. She opened it slowly, and for a few long moments, Lance stood on the balcony, listening to the sound of voices fading and footsteps retreating. One by one, they left.

When Dr. Harris came back inside, she left the door wide open. She raised her hands to show she wasn't hiding anything. "It's just me now, Lance."

Lance stared at her, his mind still a mess of tangled thoughts. Part of him wanted to believe her, but there was another part, the darker part, that told him not to. But the condo was quiet now, and it felt different.

"Okay," he whispered, his voice barely audible. He lowered the meat pounder but didn't let go of it completely. "Now what?"

. . .

"JUST RELAX," Dr. Harris said softly, her voice calm and soothing. "Take this moment by moment."

Lance nodded, but the words felt like an anchor pulling him deeper into a sea of chaos. He couldn't think straight, his mind racing with dark memories and looming shadows. The only thing he could focus on was the need to keep her away from him. He finally entered the condo and slowly walked toward her.

But as she began to approach him, his panic surged anew. "Back the hell up!" he screamed, the raw terror in his voice cutting through the silence.

Dr. Harris froze, her eyes widening slightly as she halted in her tracks. "Lance, I'm not here to hurt you. Just take a deep breath. There's—"

"Don't come any closer!" he yelled again, his heart pounding like a war drum in his chest. He could feel the walls closing in, memories of his stepbrother's voice echoing in his mind, the words slicing through him like a knife: *Nothing you do or say will change who you are.*

Dr. Harris opened her hands, palms facing him, trying to convey her intent. "Lance, please. You need to understand—"

But the sound of her voice only triggered something deep within him. All at once, he was engulfed in a whirlwind of anger and fear. He didn't want to hear her words, didn't want to face the truth she represented. With a primal scream, he ran at her and lunged, swinging the meat pounder with all his strength.

The steel connected with a sickening thud, and blood sprayed across the room, painting the walls in crimson. Lance stood frozen for a moment, the weight of what he'd done crashing down around him. Dr. Harris gasped, her eyes wide with shock and pain as she fell to the floor, crumpling like a rag doll.

Just as reality began to settle in, a gunshot rang out from somewhere behind him, the deafening sound reverberating through the space. Lance dropped the meat pounder, the weapon clattering to the floor as he instinctively stumbled backward. His heart raced as he turned, his eyes wide, looking for the source of the gunfire.

He glanced over at his shoulder, horrified to see red blossoming across the fabric, spreading like ink in water. "No...no, no, no," he murmured, panic seeping into his veins. He felt the world tilt on its axis, his body swaying as adrenaline coursed through him.

"Police! Get on the ground!" A commanding voice shouted as several officers stormed through the open front door, their guns drawn, faces taut with urgency.

Lance's mind was spinning. He dropped to his knees, overwhelmed by the chaos unfolding around him. He caught a glimpse of the fallen Dr. Harris, her body sprawled on the floor, blood pooling around her. "I didn't mean to!" he cried, the words spilling out in a frantic rush. "I didn't mean to!"

"Get down! Hands where I can see them!" one of the officers yelled again, and the sound of their commands echoed in Lance's head, drowning out everything else.

The realization of what had just happened crashed over him, a wave of disbelief washing away any semblance of clarity. He was spiraling, trapped in a vortex of fear, confusion, and regret.

As officers closed in, weapons aimed at him, Lance felt a odd sense of resignation settle over him. He was lost, and there was no escaping the truth now.

PART IV

MONDAY

10

ISOLATION

L ance lay strapped to the gurney, his body weighed down by the restraints as paramedics and officers maneuvered him out of the condo. The harsh fluorescent lights of the hallway streamed past him in blurry streaks as they moved, each flicker bringing a surreal sense of finality to everything.

Outside, the scene was chaos. Flashing red and blue lights from police cars and the SWAT truck painted the night with an eerie glow, casting long shadows that danced over the concrete. News vans had already lined the curb, their satellite dishes aimed toward the sky, and reporters strained against the crowd control barriers, microphones ready. A small crowd had gathered, phones raised, faces blurred with shock, curiosity, and horror.

As they wheeled him toward the ambulance, Lance felt a strange, almost electric thrill surge through him. He could hear snippets of whispers and gasps, could see the flashing bulbs of cameras capturing his battered face, his stained clothes. The world around him seemed so far away, yet so intimately close. In his dazed state, it all felt oddly comforting—like a stage built just for him, a twisted symphony playing only for his descent.

He let out a slow, delirious laugh, a smile stretching across his face. "They're all here for me," he murmured, voice barely a whisper, his eyes half-lidded and unfocused. "Guess I finally made it, huh?"

A paramedic glanced down, eyes sharp with concern. "Stay with me, Lance. We're taking you to the hospital. Just keep breathing."

But Lance hardly heard him. He was adrift, floating somewhere between reality and illusion. The lines had blurred too much, the echoes of his own fractured mind too loud to ignore. Each light, each face in the crowd became a hazy mosaic, shifting and reforming in shapes he could no longer make sense of. He didn't know if he was awake or dreaming, and, in that moment, he didn't care. The outside world, the murmurs of concern, the tight restraints—none of it felt real anymore.

As the ambulance doors closed, Lance caught one last look at the faces beyond the glass, his broken smile lingering. The doors slammed shut, and with it, the last shred of his tether to the world he once knew.

Inside the ambulance, as the vehicle roared to life and sped down the streets, the paramedics worked quickly, trying to stabilize him, to ground him back in reality. But Lance simply closed his eyes, sinking deeper into the comforting darkness, letting it wash over him like a final, numbing release.

Two Weeks Later

The day Lance was transferred, they ushered him into a sterile room with two chairs, a small table, and a single window offering a glimpse of the outside world he no longer felt part of. His psychiatrist, Dr. Morgan, was a tall man with sharp eyes that seemed to dissect every part of him. His therapist, Ms. Reeves, had a softer presence, her tone calm and careful, as if one wrong word might tip him over the edge. They introduced themselves, and Dr. Morgan launched into questions, blunt and probing, about his past, his outburst, and his memories—digging at things Lance had long since buried. Ms. Reeves, on the other hand, sat quietly, watching him with a gentle intensity that felt unnervingly close, as if she could see every crack in his armor. As the session dragged on, Lance's patience thinned, his pulse quickening with every invasive question.

Lance's time at the mental hospital only got worse. Settling down in his assigned room was a rough task and the routine he needed to follow? Even harder.

IT HAD HAPPENED SO FAST. Lance could still feel the shock and heat of it pulsing through him, like a live wire pressed under his skin. The patient—a quiet, older man with a nervous habit of pacing—had brushed past him in the common room, bumping his shoulder. That was all it took. Something inside Lance snapped, as if the man's touch had flipped a switch he'd been fighting to keep off. Lance had lunged, fists flying, the room blurring around him as he unleashed every bit of fury he'd been holding back. He remembered the other patient's face, frozen in horror, then the way his fists had connected, over and over, until guards swarmed in, dragging him away as he thrashed and shouted.

· · ·

LANCE SAT IN THE COLD, cramped room, every inch of it silent except for the faint hum of the fluorescent light flickering overhead. The walls were blank, gray, and close enough that he could feel them pressing in, squeezing him. Isolation. Four days, they'd said, to help him "relax and reflect." They might as well have called it a cage.

He didn't mind the loneliness at first. In a way, it felt familiar, comforting even. He'd grown up learning how to survive within himself, to keep all the fears and the anger buried deep down. But after the first day, something inside him started to itch—a need to move, to break free, to escape the stifling silence that had settled over him like a second skin. He began pacing the small space, counting the steps between the walls over and over until he could have traced them blindfolded. His breathing turned shallow, his hands clenching and unclenching as he tried to keep a lid on the restless energy building inside.

By the third day, the darkness seemed to thicken around him, like it was alive, whispering to him. Memories he'd tried to keep buried rose to the surface, faces he'd tried to forget haunting him. The taunts, the laughter, the broken promises. They circled him, mocking, reminding him of every hurt, every betrayal. He could almost feel the weight of his stepbrother's presence pressing on his shoulders, that suffocating mix of fear and shame tightening around his throat. Lance shivered, his fingers digging into his arms as he tried to ground himself, to keep from falling into the abyss that seemed to open beneath his feet.

The walls started to feel closer, the air thinner. He could barely see anything in the dim room, but the shapes of shadows seemed to twist and shift, morphing into figures that loomed over him, silent and watchful. He knew they weren't real—knew it was just the dark playing tricks on him—but that didn't make them any less terrifying. The isolation was supposed to calm him, to break the anger that had led him to lash out at another patient. Instead, it stoked the darkness inside him, feeding it until it felt like it would swallow him whole.

He started talking to himself, just to hear something other than the maddening silence. Whispered fragments of thoughts slipped out, half-formed sentences, pieces of memories. He muttered under his breath, a low, desperate sound that filled the small room like a storm barely contained.

"You're better than this," he whispered, fists clenched. "They don't know you...don't understand..."

But his own words felt empty, hollow. The rage that simmered inside him had nowhere to go, trapped in the tight confines of the cell. It scratched at his insides, a dull, aching burn that grew stronger with every passing hour. He slammed his fist against the wall, the pain shooting up his arm a brief, satisfying release.

By the time the fourth day dawned, Lance was hanging by a thread.

11

SELF

L ance returned to his assigned room, swallowing the pills they handed him without question— medication to keep him dull, to quiet the storm inside. Days blurred into one another, gray and weightless, until one afternoon in the courtyard something shifted. He noticed a little boy standing alone near a cluster of trees, facing away. Lance squinted, unsure if his mind was playing tricks on him, but the boy's silhouette felt strangely familiar.

He approached cautiously, his heart pounding against the fog of his medication. Step by step, the boy came into clearer view—a small figure with messy hair and a slight slouch, the way he remembered himself at that age. Lance stopped, his mouth dry, struggling to breathe as he reached out and tapped the boy's shoulder. Slowly, the boy turned, and Lance felt like the ground had dropped from under him.

It was him—his own face, staring back, young and fragile, carrying an expression of quiet fear that Lance knew too well. The boy's gaze held a sadness that ran deeper than his years, an unspoken pain that mirrored the dark corners of

Lance's mind. The child stared up at him, as if recognizing the man he'd become, his lips pressed tight, saying nothing.

Lance's chest tightened. "Are you real?" he whispered, barely audible, his voice thick with desperation. But the boy only blinked, expression unreadable, then turned and began to walk away, his small figure slipping back toward the trees.

"Wait!" Lance choked out, taking a step forward, his body heavy with a strange paralysis. But the boy kept moving, drifting further into the shadows, leaving Lance rooted in place, haunted by the image of himself slipping away.

AFTERWORD

There's a part of each of us, hidden beneath the polished words and measured expressions, that we don't often show the world. It's the darkness we rarely even name out loud, the side of us that simmers with raw, unfiltered emotion. Anger, fear, shame—the things we work so hard to cope against. But that shadowed part of ourselves doesn't just disappear. It waits, and it watches, and it grows stronger the longer we ignore it.

Therapy helps, sure. Talking to friends helps, too. But there are pieces we still hold back, even in those spaces. Why? Maybe it's because we're afraid of being judged, or maybe we're afraid of what that part of us really says about who we are. There's a primal side, a shadow self, that knows our deepest insecurities, our darkest fears, and every fractured thought we hide from the light. We keep it hidden because it's messy, it's ugly, and sometimes it even scares us.

But here's the truth: until we face that inner darkness, until we bring it to light and recognize it as part of who we are, we're always going to feel like something's missing. The shadow self isn't something to be erased; it's a part of us that needs acknowledgment, understanding, maybe even compassion. Because ignoring it—pretending it's not there —only strengthens its grip. And when it finally finds a way out, it often comes in ways we can't control.

Lance's story is a reflection of what happens when that part of us is left unchecked, unexamined. We all have a breaking point, a place where denial or avoidance turns to chaos, and that chaos can spiral into something unthinkable. Lance didn't face his inner darkness; he ran from it, and eventually, it consumed him. That's the danger—when we don't face our shadows, they start to make decisions for us.

So maybe the challenge isn't to silence the darkness but to listen to it. To let it speak, without fear or judgment, and to try to understand it. Because once we do, it loses its power over us. We reclaim ourselves, piece by piece, by daring to explore the very things that make us uncomfortable. And when we bring them into the light, we can finally start to heal.

ABOUT THE AUTHOR

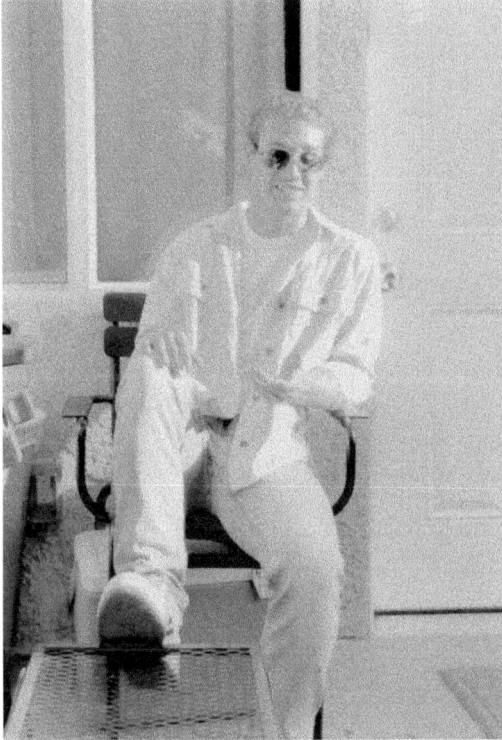

Nicholas Michael Matiz is a bold voice in the realm of Gay fiction, known for his gritty, raw storytelling that pushes boundaries and explores the darker sides of human nature.

ALSO BY NICHOLAS MICHAEL MATIZ

Fading Into Silence

Out of the Closet

The Lonely Road*

www.ingramcontent.com/pod-product-compliance
Ingram Content Group UK Ltd.
Pitfield, Milton Keynes, MK11 3LW, UK
UKHW021009280325
456847UK00007B/925